The Rescue Princesses

The Secret Promise

More amazing
animal adventures!

The Wishing Pearl

The Moonlight Mystery

The Stolen Crystals

The Rescue Princesses

The Secret Promise

♥ PAULA HARRISON ♥

Scholastic Inc.

No part of this publication may be reproduced, stored in a retrieval system, or transmitted in any form or by any means, electronic, mechanical, photocopying, recording, or otherwise, without written permission of the publisher. For information regarding permission, write to Nosy Crow Ltd., The Crow's Nest, 10a Lant Street, London, SE1 1QR, UK.

ISBN 978-0-545-50913-8

Text copyright © 2012 by Paula Harrison
Interior illustrations copyright © 2012 by Artful Doodlers

All rights reserved. Published by Scholastic Inc., 557 Broadway, New York, NY 10012, by arrangement with Nosy Crow Ltd.

SCHOLASTIC and associated logos are trademarks and/or registered trademarks of Scholastic Inc. NOSY CROW and associated logos are trademarks and/or registered trademarks of Nosy Crow Ltd.

12 11 10 9 8 7 6 5 4 3   13 14 15 16 17 18/0

Printed in the U.S.A.   40

First printing, June 2013

For Abby and Megan, true Princesses,
with all my love

CHAPTER ONE

The Castle of Mistberg Forest

Princess Emily leaned out of the carriage window, trying to get her first glimpse of the famous castle of Mistberg Forest.

She'd waited nine years for her chance to visit and she couldn't wait a second longer. The forest air swept over her, sending her crown slipping sideways and her red curls flapping.

"Emily! Please don't hang your head out of the window like that. It doesn't look very graceful," said her mom, straightening her own crown.

Princess Emily took one last look and reluctantly pulled her head back in. "You should have let me drive. I could have gone much faster than this."

Her dad's mouth twitched into a smile.

"The point is to arrive in royal style," said her mom. "Not to shoot along like a race car."

Emily resisted saying that racing would have been more fun. Her mom and dad were the king and queen of Middingland, and they always knew the right way to do things.

They had flown across the sea from Middingland that morning in the royal jet. Then they had traveled from the airport in a carriage, because everyone arrived at the Mistberg Grand Ball by horse and carriage. The ball took place

at King Gudland's castle every spring and was one of the biggest events of the season.

The scent of pine trees filled the carriage, and Emily caught a flash of movement as a deer ran deeper into the forest. The horses pulling the carriage slowed down to a walk as they passed through gigantic golden gates.

The call of a peacock echoed across the grass. Emily held her breath. *We must be inside the grounds of the castle!* She stuck her head out of the window again, and her heart drummed with excitement.

"When we get inside we have a dress fitting at two o'clock," said the queen. "Please remember to brush your hair, Emily. It's gotten a little wild in the breeze."

But Emily wasn't thinking about brushing her hair. Above her towered the round turrets of King Gudland's castle, stretching up to the sky.

Usually her little sister would have nudged her out of the way, but Lottie was staying with their cousins to recover from a bout of chickenpox, so, for once, Emily had a perfect view.

The castle was much more magnificent than their palace in Middingland, and she had three whole days to explore it.

A short, white-haired man hurried down the flight of steps as the carriage drew to a halt.

"Philip! Maria! How wonderful to see you!" he exclaimed.

"Hermann, how are you?" said Emily's mom, gracefully stepping down from the carriage. She turned to her daughter. "Emily, I'd like you to meet King Gudland."

"A pleasure to meet you, Princess," said King Gudland.

Emily curtsied. She instantly liked the small man with twinkly eyes. She hoped all the other kings and queens were as friendly as he was.

The purpose of the Mistberg Grand Ball was for young princes and princesses, age nine or older, to present themselves to the twenty royal families from around the world.

Emily had never been there before because her parents had been so busy with their royal duties at home in the kingdom of Middingland. But this year was different; Emily was old enough now to take part in the ceremony.

In three days she would have to curtsy in front of each and every king and queen, and she was already a little nervous.

"Come this way, Your Majesties," said King Gudland. He led them through an enormous hallway full of people hurrying around with suitcases.

They climbed up five spiraling staircases, watched by the solemn pictures of King Gudland's ancestors. When they reached the top, the king waved his hand toward three wooden doors.

"This is the West Tower, with my most comfortable rooms," he said. "The banquet begins at six o'clock. Don't be late!" He gave Emily another twinkly smile before stepping back down the staircase.

"That's your room, Emily," said her mom, pointing to the first door. "Meet me in the dressmaking suite in half an hour. It's two staircases down and then on the right. You can't miss it."

Emily nodded, pushed her door open, and took her first look at her room. A four-poster bed filled one corner, and a soft, velvety sofa sat in the other. But Emily was drawn to the window, and when she got closer she realized that she was very close to the top of the tower.

Everything on the ground looked tiny. She could see the stables for King Gudland's horses and a set of obstacles that looked like a huge adventure playground.

As she stared down, another carriage pulled up in front of the castle and a girl dressed in green climbed out.

Emily watched her eagerly. She was looking forward to meeting some more princesses her own age. Life at home in her palace in Middingland was great, but there was only her little sister to play with.

Suddenly, Emily looked at her watch. Half an hour had flown by while she was daydreaming at the window. She was supposed to be in the dressmaking suite with her mom right now!

She rushed out of her room and back to the staircase. What had her mom said? Two staircases down? Yes, that was it.

She raced down the two sets of spiral steps so fast that she began to feel dizzy. At the bottom, she stopped, looking left, then right. Which one was it?

Emily turned left. There was only one door in the passageway. That must have been why Mom had said she wouldn't miss it.

As she opened the door, she heard a man's deep voice. It sounded as cold as glass.

"There must be absolute secrecy, you understand? I will not put up with ridiculous mistakes," said the voice.

"Yes, My Lord. We understand," came the reply.

Emily stopped uncertainly. The man with the deep voice had his back to her. She could tell he was very rich by the fancy dark cape and purple hat he wore. The two other men nodded their heads humbly, their eyes fixed on the rich man.

This wasn't the dressmaking suite. She must have turned the wrong way. Emily started to tiptoe backward. But the man with the deep voice turned around.

"What do you think you're doing? Come back right now!" he barked, striding toward her.

Emily knew she had no explanation good enough for a man who barked like that. Spinning around, she ran back to the stairwell, her feet thudding across the red carpet.

She rushed down the opposite hallway, tearing open the first door and landing inside the dressmaking suite in a tangle of arms and legs.

CHAPTER TWO

The Other Princesses

"Emily!" Her mom's face froze in a frown. "Why on earth are you charging around like this?"

"I went the wrong way." Emily gasped. "When I opened the door there was a —" She stopped, suddenly aware of all the eyes that were fixed on her.

Three other princesses stood nearby with their moms, while dressmakers fussed around them with pins and tape measures.

Emily picked herself up, feeling shy.

"Well, never mind," said Queen Maria with a sigh. "Now that you're finally here, please come and try this dress on. We have to make sure it fits correctly for the Grand Ball on Saturday."

Emily followed her into the middle of the room. There were mirrors everywhere, and long shelves stretched all the way along one wall.

The highest shelf was covered with gold and silver necklaces. The middle one was full of shiny satin gloves, and the lowest shelf had rows of party shoes covered in glittering stones.

Emily looked longingly at the necklaces. She'd brought her own ruby necklace in her suitcase, but she knew her mom would make her save it until the night of the Grand Ball.

She went into a changing room and

pulled the dress over her head. It was a pink ball gown made of smooth satin and decorated with red flowers.

When she came out and looked in a mirror, her heart leapt. This dress was the most beautiful one she'd ever had. Her long red hair curled over the satin material and her hazel eyes shone brightly.

"Stand up really straight, please, Emily," said her mom, fastening the buttons at the back. "Now remember, we're saving this for the very last evening, so that you can wear it to the Grand Ball."

Emily took the opportunity to have a look at the other princesses. The girl closest to her was the same one she'd seen getting out of the carriage earlier.

She had dark hair and serious brown eyes, and wore a green silk dress. She saw Emily looking her way and smiled back.

The next girl stood gracefully, with long golden hair falling down her back. Her mom was checking the fit of her pale-blue dress, which was so long that it even hid her feet.

The girl farthest away from Emily had dark eyes and black hair. She wore a bright-yellow dress dotted with sequins. She saw Emily looking at her.

"Hi, I'm Lulu from the kingdom of Undala, near the Great Desert," she said with a wide grin.

"I'm Emily from Middingland," said Emily, smiling back. "It's great to meet you."

"I'm Jaminta, from Onica, by the Silver River," said the girl in green.

"And I'm Clarabel," said the blond-haired girl, smiling shyly, "from the kingdom of Winteria, in the cold North."

"When did you —" started Emily.

"Girls!" scolded Lulu's mom. "There'll be lots of time for chatting later. Hold still now, Lulu. We need to measure you for your velvet cloak."

"Thank goodness you mentioned that! I nearly forgot," said Emily's mom. "Every princess needs a cloak to wear at Mistberg Castle. Turn around, Emily, while I check how long it should be."

The princesses exchanged grins as they lapsed back into silence.

Emily looked at herself in the mirror. The dress looked great already. She didn't really want to hide it under a cloak.

From outside the window came loud whoops and yells. Her mom was still holding the tape measure against her dress, so Emily tried to lean over to peer into the garden without moving her feet.

Right outside the window was the obstacle course that she'd seen from her tower window. Now that she was on a lower floor she could see it much more clearly.

Four young princes were playing on the equipment, climbing the ropes, swinging across the monkey bars, and flying down the zip line.

As Emily watched them, she longed to be out there. "Mom!" she cried, trying to wriggle free. "Have you finished measuring for the cloak yet? I really want a go on that obstacle course."

"There'll be plenty of time for that later," said Queen Maria.

"Your Highness, we haven't given you all the necessary instructions yet," said the head dressmaker. "All young princesses must know the correct manners for the Grand Ball. How to enter the Banquet Hall and curtsy in the right place. How to hold your head straight as you walk. How to place yourself on your seat correctly at the start of the meal. There are many things to practice this afternoon."

Emily sighed. The other princesses didn't look very happy, either.

"I think I know how to sit down on a chair," muttered Lulu. But she fell silent after a look from her mom, the queen of Undala.

Emily looked from the zip line to her mom, who was still fiddling with the tape measure. She sighed. It was going to be a *very* long afternoon.

💜

Emily got back to her turret bedroom as the sun began to set. She found her maid, Ally, taking things out of her suitcase and putting them away.

Ally looked at her. "What's that frown for?" she asked immediately.

Emily smiled. Ally had been her maid since she was five and could read her moods easily.

"We had to do lots of silly stuff like practice walking and curtsying," said Emily. "Mom said I could go outside when we finished but there wasn't time, and now I have to go to the banquet. I'd really love to try out that zip line."

"Well, maybe you still can. If you choose the moment carefully, you could go out for a little while without them missing you," said Ally, picking up a pair of glittery silver shoes and putting them in the wardrobe.

Emily looked thoughtful. Ally always told her to work hard at her princess duties, but also liked her to think for herself. Everyone has a brain and everyone should use it, she always said.

Before she became Emily's maid, Ally had spent several years working as an undercover agent, solving jewel robberies and catching thieves.

Emily sometimes wondered if her maid had really wanted to give up her old job, but Ally would always just say that she was happy working in the palace.

"I know! I'll go out there after we finish eating. No one will miss me then," said Emily.

"Be careful," warned Ally. "You should take a flashlight with you; it's getting dark."

Emily put on a cherry-red dress for the banquet. She added a gold tiara and a gold necklace, which she'd been allowed to borrow from the dressmaking room.

Her heart began to thump faster. Now sitting and listening to the grown-ups' boring conversations wouldn't seem so bad. She wouldn't mind the curtsying or the endless fussing with napkins. Not now that her own adventure was only a few moments away.

CHAPTER THREE

Climbing in the Dark

Crystal chandeliers lit up the enormous Banquet Hall and rich tapestries lined the walls. Emily gazed around in amazement, her gold tiara sparkling on top of her red curls.

Over her dress she wore the black velvet cloak her mom had chosen for her. Her stomach rumbled as delicious dinner smells drifted through from the kitchens.

The kings and queens of the twenty royal families from all around the world were bowing and chatting with one another. The empress of the Marica Isles swept by, wearing a coral necklace that swung grandly from her neck.

The king of Undala, looking very regal in his golden turban, bowed low to Queen Trudy of Leepland, who gave him a sharp nod. At her side, she clutched a boy with a sulky expression wearing an orange vest.

Emily sat down at the banquet table next to her mom and dad. She knew who all the kings and queens were because she'd been studying them in her lessons for weeks. But she was thankful that she didn't have to start talking and curtsying to them all yet. The Grand Ball would take place in two days' time. Until then, she was happy to stay in the background.

"Emily, please remove your elbows from the table," whispered her mom.

Emily took her elbows off and tried to sit up straight. It was harder than it looked. She gazed across the Banquet Hall and suddenly felt her shoulders tighten.

At a far table sat the man with the deep voice and purple hat who'd shouted at her earlier. Luckily, he wasn't looking at her. He was smiling at the person sitting next to him, the twinkly-eyed King Gudland. He didn't look as fierce now, although Emily still hoped she wouldn't run into him again anytime soon.

Queen Maria leaned toward her. "As well as meeting the other princesses, you'll see some princes here that are your age. Look, there's Prince Olaf of Finia."

Emily glanced at the tall, blond-haired boy from Finia, then she noticed the boy with the sulky face again.

"Who's the prince wearing orange, next to the queen of Leepland?" whispered Emily, wondering why he looked so grumpy.

"Mom? Why can't I have dessert first?" whined the boy. "You always let me at home."

"That's her son, Prince Samuel," said her mom quietly. "Now, remember, Emily! Use the silverware from the outside first and chew slowly."

Emily stared at the huge spread of knives, forks, and spoons next to her plate. *Use the ones on the outside first*, she thought. Why was there always so much to remember?

A gong sounded to signal the start of the meal. The food tasted wonderful, but Emily's feet tapped impatiently. When could she slip out? Did she have to wait until every single person had finished?

Finally, dessert was served. Bowls of chocolate pudding and tall ice-cream sundaes were soon emptied, and the grown-ups began to murmur about having coffee in the drawing room.

Emily sprang up. "I'll be back in a minute," she said to her mom.

Queen Maria nodded. Emily hurried out of the hall, down the passageway, and past the kitchens to the back door.

Her hand gripped the flashlight that she'd tucked underneath her cloak. Afraid of being caught at the last moment, she rushed straight out the door and into the night.

She felt small in the darkness. Switching on the light, she let the round beam travel over the garden. She tried to remember how everything had looked in daylight.

Over to one side was the fountain and the maze. She followed the gravel path to a wide courtyard set out with chairs and tables. Then she hurried down a slope and there, beyond the lawn, stood the biggest obstacle course she'd ever seen.

She raced over to it, the beam of her flashlight bouncing as she ran. Where would she start? The zip line, of course!

She climbed up the long ladder to the high platform, tucked the flashlight back in her pocket, and grabbed ahold of the rope. The thought of flying down there in the dark gave her a bubbly feeling in her stomach, half excited and half scared.

She couldn't even *see* the other end of the zip line; it was too far away in the shadows. Her skirts rustled around her as she got ready to leap off the platform.

Oh! She'd nearly forgotten! She couldn't go on the zip line wearing the huge cloak. It would only slow her down.

She pulled the cloak off and laid it over the wooden railing behind her. Then, taking the rope in both hands, she jumped.

The darkness rushed past her. She swooped down the line, feet dangling, until she felt the crash as the bar hit the other end and her legs swung up. Then she plunged backward, slowing down steadily until her feet hit the ground.

Emily let go of the rope, grinning widely. She'd loved that; it was just like flying.

"That was awesome!" A girl came closer, her blond hair and blue dress glimmering in the light spilling from the castle windows.

"Princess Clarabel?" asked Emily.

Clarabel nodded. "Yes, it's me. I came out to look at the obstacle course. I can't believe you went all the way down there in the dark."

"It was amazing!" said Emily. "Are you going to try it?"

"I might." Clarabel chewed her lip. "Maybe I'll see how fast it goes first."

"Woo-hoo!" A yell came out of the darkness.

Emily spun around, grabbing for her flashlight and shining it into the air. A figure in yellow climbed up the cargo net and swung herself over the top.

"Princess Lulu conquers the world!" she shouted, scrambling down the other side.

Emily and Clarabel burst out laughing.

One last figure came running down the slope, a dazzling green light fixed to her arm. "Am I missing all the fun?" said Princess Jaminta.

Emily stared at her wrist. "What's that?" she asked.

Jaminta held out her arm to show Emily the bracelet that glowed far brighter than her flashlight.

"It's made of emeralds. I found a way to make jewels work like gadgets," said Jaminta. "I can give them power or make them warm. Or I can make them light up just like this. I like using emeralds best."

"That's incredible!" said Emily admiringly.

"Ooh, I wish you could make my jewel glow," said Clarabel, touching the dark-blue sapphire that hung from a chain around her neck.

Lulu came running over, landing in front of them with a double-flip somersault. "I guess none of us could bear sitting still in that hall a second longer," she said, grinning. "So, who's next on the zip line?"

"Let's race for it!" said Emily.

They raced to the ladder, laughing as they ran. Lulu reached it first. She pulled herself up and the others followed. Climbing up last, Clarabel looked a little worried as she peered down at the ground.

When they all stood on the platform at the top, Emily said, "Should we try going down it two at a time?"

But just then a screeching noise came out of the night. It sent tingles down Emily's neck.

"What was that? It sounded horrible!" exclaimed Lulu.

"That was a distress call," said Clarabel. "The sound of an animal in trouble."

"It came from out there in the forest," added Jaminta, shining her emerald bracelet in that direction.

"We should go and find it," said Emily. "We might be able to help."

"It's very dark," said Clarabel nervously. "But you're right, some poor animal needs us."

"Let's go!" said Lulu.

The girls climbed swiftly back down the ladder and ran across the garden. They passed through the castle gates in a whirl of colored dresses and rushed out into the forest beyond.

CHAPTER FOUR

The Dark Forest

Emily ran between the trees, glad that the other princesses were beside her.

It was much darker out here beyond the castle walls. Low branches reached down to catch them and Emily had to stop and untangle herself.

"Do you think we're going the right way?" she asked.

"Listen," said Clarabel. "I think I heard it again."

They stopped for a moment, trying to hear the animal noise over the wind blowing and the swooshing of the leaves.

"There it is," said Lulu.

The half-crying, half-grunting noise sounded much weaker now. The princesses ran toward it, slowing down as the ground became thick with tree roots and brambles.

On the earth lay a young deer with one leg bent at an awkward angle. The animal turned its black eyes on them, trembling with fright. Emily caught the glint of something silver on the ground.

"Look! It's caught in something," she said.

Clarabel knelt down next to the deer. "Poor thing! No wonder it made that horrible noise."

"That looks like a man-made trap," said Jaminta grimly.

"Why would anyone trap an animal like this?" said Clarabel. "I'm sure it's not allowed."

"King Gudland doesn't seem like the sort of king who would let this happen," agreed Emily. "How are we going to set it free?"

Jaminta bent down to look more closely at the metal teeth of the trap. The emeralds on her wrist cast a bright-green light over everything. Clarabel spoke soothingly to the deer, trying to calm down the shivering animal.

"The trap's clamped really tightly around its foot. It won't be easy to release it," said Jaminta. "Even if we manage to open it, the deer still won't be able to walk."

"Just get that trap open!" said Lulu. "I've got an idea." She turned and sprinted away through the forest.

Jaminta pulled a small screwdriver out of her dress pocket. "Could you keep its leg really still?" she said to Emily.

Emily nodded and held on to the deer's leg firmly, its brown coat feeling velvety beneath her hands. The creature quivered, its huge black eyes opening wide with fear.

"Don't worry," whispered Clarabel, stroking between its ears. "We'll have you free in no time." The young animal turned its soft nose toward her and its ears twitched. It almost seemed as if it knew what she was saying.

Jaminta worked quickly, loosening four screws on the trap, one after the other. The deer squirmed and Emily struggled to keep it still. She kept a tight hold on the leg, praying that Jaminta could work magic with her screwdriver and get the trap undone.

"Stay still, little one," murmured Clarabel.

Jaminta twisted the screws looser, one by one. "Almost there," she said.

The deer wriggled harder, and for a moment Emily thought she would lose her grip on its leg.

"That's it!" Jaminta pulled out the last screw and stuck the screwdriver behind her ear.

Emily pulled the trap open, keeping her fingers away from its sharp silver teeth. Gently she lifted out the deer's leg.

"Look! There's no cut here at all," she said. "Maybe this little deer just fell badly when the trap closed."

"Luckily, it's young and its small leg fit right between the teeth of the trap. Otherwise its injuries would have been much worse," said Jaminta.

Suddenly, Lulu arrived, crashing

through the branches with a wheelbarrow. "Great! You got the trap open," she said breathlessly.

The deer began shivering again, its wide eyes fixed on Lulu.

But Lulu didn't notice. "I found this in the greenhouse." She pointed at the wheelbarrow. "We can use it to take the deer back to the castle."

"We have to be really quiet, though. It's still very frightened." Clarabel put her arms around the animal. "It's going to need a lot of looking after and it's going to take a while for that leg to heal."

"Let's lift it into the wheelbarrow, on three," said Emily. "One, two, three . . ."

They lifted the deer, which was surprisingly heavy, and set it down inside the wheelbarrow. Clarabel stroked the creature's soft ears until it became still and quiet, as if it sensed it was in good hands.

Emily and Lulu took one side of the wheelbarrow each, while Jaminta and Clarabel went on ahead, lighting the way with Jaminta's glowing bracelet. They wheeled the deer past the golden gates, onto the grounds, and right up to the castle.

"Let's put the deer somewhere safe for tonight and tell the grown-ups about it in the morning," said Emily. "They won't want to hear about it right now, while the banquet's still going on."

Clarabel nodded. "Good idea."

"There's a shed next to the greenhouse," said Lulu. "It will be fine in there."

Jaminta marched over to the castle windows and peered in. "Looks like they're still having their coffee."

Emily shrugged her shoulders. "They're so busy chatting I bet they didn't even hear the deer making that loud cry."

They settled the deer down in the garden shed. Clarabel found some straw for it to lie on and covered its legs with an old blanket that she found on a shelf. Lulu pulled some cabbages out of the garden and left them nearby in case it got hungry during the night.

The deer watched them, its big dark eyes no longer frightened. Finally, it rested its head on one side and its breathing grew slow and steady.

Emily quietly closed the shed door and the four princesses looked at one another. Their tiaras glittered in the green light from Jaminta's bracelet, and their eyes shone as bright as stars.

"I can't believe we went into the forest in the dark," said Clarabel.

Lulu smiled. "And now you've got a leaf on your tiara."

Clarabel brushed off the leaf, then she

laughed. "You've got a huge twig sticking out of yours!"

"Oops!" Lulu grinned.

Emily picked the twig off Lulu's tiara for her. Then she turned to Jaminta. "I think your bracelet's really cool."

"Thanks. I'd really like to make some more," said Jaminta. "I've got plans for what else I can do. I'll show you all tomorrow."

"Let's meet up before breakfast," said Lulu.

"Good idea. We should show King Gudland right away where we've put the deer," said Emily, smiling at her new friends. "If we tell him about the trap together, he'll have to listen. After all, princesses should stick together. No matter what."

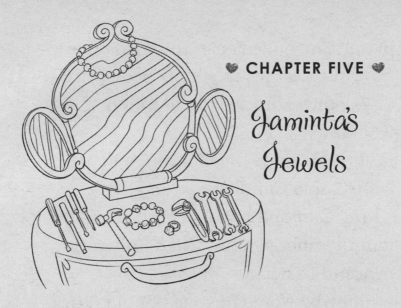

CHAPTER FIVE

Jaminta's Jewels

The four princesses dragged King
Gudland down to the garden shed the
following morning, telling him all about
their deer on the way.

They had dressed quickly, throwing
on dresses and plain silver tiaras. The
morning sun beamed across the garden
and made the tops of the castle turrets
sparkle.

"We put it in here, Your Majesty,"
explained Lulu. "It seemed like a safe

place." She pulled open the shed door to show the deer resting on its bed of straw.

"Goodness gracious!" said King Gudland.

"It needs some time for its leg to get better," said Clarabel.

King Gudland nodded. "You've put it in the right place. It will be nice and peaceful in here."

"But why would anyone put out a trap for animals? It's such a horrible thing to do," said Emily.

"Trapping is forbidden in Mistberg Forest," said the king. "Maybe you were mistaken. Maybe the deer tripped on a branch."

Emily's mom and dad arrived. They'd seen them from across the garden.

"Girls!" interrupted Emily's dad. "Leave the king alone now. We haven't even had breakfast yet."

"But . . ." Emily wanted to mention the trap again, but the grown-ups were already turning away.

"Good morning, Your Majesties!" said a whiny voice. Prince Samuel, dressed in his orange vest, walked over to them. He held a straggly piece of damp material out at arm's length, as if it was something disgusting.

Emily looked at the material and her stomach lurched. She had a feeling there was something she'd forgotten. Something important.

"I found this at the top of the zip line," said the prince with a smirk. "I just wondered if it belonged to anyone."

"Emily!" cried her mom. "Is that your cloak?"

Emily grabbed the soggy cloak from the prince. "I must have left it there last night."

"Thank you, Prince Samuel," said Emily's mom. "Emily, I would like to talk to you!"

"You said I could go on the obstacle course," said Emily. "I just forgot about the cloak."

Queen Maria shook her head. "Of course you're allowed on the climbing equipment. Exercise is good for you. But honestly, Emily! You're not supposed to run off and play in the middle of a banquet!"

"I'm sorry," said Emily. "I only planned to be gone for a minute."

"You need to put your princess duties first. Remember what you should be doing and look after your belongings properly."

Emily sighed. "Yes, Mom."

The queen's face softened into a smile. "Let's go back inside. I hear the cook is serving blueberry muffins for breakfast."

Luckily, the rest of the day was free from curtsying practice, although Emily had to take her wet cloak down to the laundry room to be cleaned.

The princesses spent some time after breakfast feeding their deer. Then they gathered in Jaminta's room in the East Tower.

Jaminta's four-poster bed was draped with shimmering green and gold cloth. Her dressing table was covered with silver tools all neatly lined up, including a small screwdriver and a chisel.

"I can't wait to see these amazing jewels," said Emily.

"They're very special," replied Jaminta. "Where I come from, by the Silver River near the Eastern Mountains, we love to

collect precious stones. If you chisel them into shape correctly, you can use them in all kinds of ways."

She pulled the curtains across the window to darken the room and put a large gold jewelry box down on the bed. The other princesses leaned in closer.

"These are the ones that give out light." Jaminta carefully pulled back the lid. Light burst from the shining jewels in all the colors of the rainbow. They lit up the dark room, making it seem like a cave full of treasure.

"Wow!" cried the princesses.

"Now I'm trying to see what else I can do with them. See!" Jaminta opened a smaller jewelry box, picked out a round ruby, and put it into the palm of Emily's hand. The jewel rested there, gradually warming up until Emily felt like she was holding a little ball of fire.

"It's so warm. It could definitely come in handy in winter," said Emily.

"That's good," said Clarabel. "It gets so cold in Winteria, where I come from."

"No need for extra heat in Undala," joked Lulu. "Our grasslands bake in the hot sun."

"Well, I haven't invented a jewel that cools you down," said Jaminta with a laugh. "Not yet, anyway!"

Clarabel smiled. "I don't think we would have found the deer last night without your bracelet. It was so bright."

"King Gudland didn't believe us about the trap, though," said Emily. "He thought we were mistaken."

Jaminta frowned. "It was definitely a man-made trap. It took me forever to get all those screws undone."

Emily looked thoughtful. "If the king doesn't believe us, then maybe we should go out and find the trap and bring it back to show him. Then he can look for the people who left it."

"Great idea!" said Lulu, and the others nodded.

"Let's hurry," said Emily. "The sooner we show the trap to King Gudland, the sooner we can prove that we were telling the truth about the deer all along."

CHAPTER SIX

Meeting the Princes

Jaminta put her jewels away and the princesses headed out into the sunshine. On the way, they collected King Gudland's dog, Denny, because they had offered to take him for a walk.

They also charmed a picnic basket out of the cook, stuffed with sandwiches, slices of chocolate cake, and a container of strawberries.

As they walked across the garden, they spotted the four princes playing on the obstacle course again. Emily recognized Prince Samuel, the boy who'd handed her soggy cloak back to her that morning.

"Hey!" called the tallest prince. "What are you guys doing?"

"Going for a walk," Lulu yelled back, and the princesses kept moving.

The tall prince, who had a head of ruffled blond hair, ran over to them. "I'm Olaf, from the kingdom of Finia. Want to race against us on the obstacle course? Princes against princesses?"

Prince Samuel snorted behind him. "That'll be easy. Princesses are *really* slow."

Lulu's eyes flashed. "You obviously haven't met princesses like us, then," she snapped.

"Are these your friends?" Emily asked Prince Olaf.

"Yes. This is George, from Carathia."

Olaf nodded to a black-eyed boy, who grinned widely. "And this is Dinesh, and he's from —"

"From Ratastan," said the short, serious-looking boy.

There was a pause and they all looked at Samuel.

"I'm Prince Samuel, from the kingdom of Leepland, the land of the most riches and the best people," said Samuel, his pale face twisting haughtily.

Prince Olaf ignored him. "How about a race?" he asked the princesses.

Emily smiled. She'd never met any of the princes before, but she instantly liked the lively Prince Olaf. She wasn't so sure about Samuel, though; she was almost positive he'd enjoyed getting her in trouble earlier.

"Maybe we can race you later," said Emily, then paused. She wondered if she should mention their plan to find the deer trap. Maybe not in front of Samuel. "We're just taking King Gudland's dog for a walk."

She was about to add that they were going into the woods, when a shrill voice drifted down from the castle.

"Samuel! I hope you aren't getting that new vest dirty!" A thin lady with a pointed nose trotted out the castle door. "Samuel! What are you doing?"

Prince Olaf nudged Samuel. "It's your mom," he hissed.

Queen Trudy sped up, glaring at the girls as she came closer. "Samuel, I hope you're being careful who you're friends with. Just look at the mud on their shoes!"

Emily didn't want to wait around to meet such a disagreeable person. She turned to the other princesses. "Let's go. We have to continue our walk."

They waved good-bye to the princes and headed off across the castle garden. Denny the dog bounded ahead of them. His tail wagged wildly and the breeze ruffled his dark-brown coat.

"Denny! Come back!" shouted Emily, dodging around a stone fountain.

She chased him past a row of high fir trees, nearly running right into a very tall man. Darting sideways, she just managed to avoid him. But then she lost her balance, fell into a tree, and got a face full of needlelike leaves.

"Aha! The red-headed princess! I was sure we would meet again," said a deep voice.

Emily recognized the man with the purple hat, whose room she'd stumbled into the day before. Her heart sank. It was the worst luck to bump into him.

"It was so nice of you to drop in

yesterday," said the man, showing his teeth.

Emily assumed it was supposed to be a smile, but she couldn't help thinking of a shark. "I didn't mean to disturb you. I went into your room by mistake," she said, jumping to her feet.

The other princesses came running up, and Denny darted around in circles barking at everyone.

The man showed a flicker of a frown when he saw the dog, but it was gone in an instant. "So where are you all off to?" he asked.

"We're going for a walk in the forest, My Lord," replied Lulu.

The frown returned. "That's not a good idea." The man paused. "It's so easy to get lost out there."

"That's okay. I have a compass to check our direction," said Jaminta, getting the

small round compass out of her pocket to show him.

"Good day to you, My Lord," said Clarabel.

All the princesses curtsied and continued across the garden.

The man didn't reply, but stood watching them, his dark eyes cast into shadow.

"Who is that?" asked Emily. "And why doesn't he want us going for a walk?"

"That's Duke Raven," Jaminta told them. "My dad told me that he lives in this kingdom and he's a cousin of King Gudland. Maybe he really thinks we'll get lost."

Ahead of them, a golden gate towered, gleaming in the sunshine. This was where the castle grounds ended and the forest began. Clarabel put Denny's leash on to stop him from running too far away.

They walked through the gateway and the trees stretched out in front of them. Shafts of sunlight drifted through the branches. Leaves rustled here and there as mice and squirrels scurried around.

"Which way to the place where we rescued the deer?" asked Lulu.

Jaminta looked around and checked her compass. "We turned right over here. So we should be heading southwest."

They walked together, searching for any glimpse of metal on the ground.

"None of this looks the same as last night," said Emily suddenly.

"Well, it *was* really dark, even with the light from Jaminta's bracelet," Lulu pointed out.

"But there were tree roots everywhere, and I can't see any here," said Emily.

Jaminta looked at her compass again. "Maybe we should spread out a little more, but not so much that we can't see each other."

The princesses spread out through the trees and continued walking in the same direction.

Emily's stomach rumbled, which made her think about the chocolate cake in the picnic basket. Then her foot hit something and she grabbed on to a tree trunk to keep herself from falling over.

"Hey!" she yelled. "There are lots of tree roots over here."

The princesses came running up.

"Yes, this looks like the right place," said Clarabel. "Remember how the deer was lying right next to the bottom of a tree?"

They searched all the trees nearby. Denny snuffled at the ground and wagged his tail excitedly.

"Look!" Clarabel pointed to a patch of ground with strange scrape marks on it.

Emily bit her lip. "Maybe this was the place. But where's the trap?"

Jaminta walked around the tree trunk, peering at the ground. She bent down next to a large footprint clearly marked in the soft forest earth. "Look at this," she said grimly. "Someone came here and took the trap with them."

"That's terrible!" snapped Lulu. "First they set the trap and now they try to pretend it was never here."

"Now we have nothing to show King Gudland," said Jaminta.

"They could come back with more traps and nobody would stop them!" cried Clarabel. "So many deer could get hurt."

"Wait!" Emily's face suddenly lit up. "Maybe *we* can stop them! I know a way we can find out secrets and move around the forest without anyone ever seeing us."

"Really? How?" asked Lulu, her lionlike eyes widening.

"We can turn into ninjas!" said Emily.

The princesses' mouths dropped open.

"Really?" said Jaminta.

"Really!" said Emily. "We can be just like ninjas, and I know who can show us how to do it."

CHAPTER SEVEN

Ninja Princesses

After checking on the deer in the shed and finding it some more food, Emily took the girls back to her room in the West Tower. The room had been cleaned and the sofa scattered with soft red cushions.

"Hey! Ally left slippers out for all of us," said Emily, wiggling her toes into red slippers dotted with diamonds. "Almost like she knew we were coming."

She handed out the jeweled slippers to

her friends: green to Jaminta, yellow to Lulu, and blue to Clarabel. Then she took one look at Clarabel's sad face and sent an order down to the kitchen for hot chocolate.

"I'm just thinking of the little deer," explained Clarabel. "What if he's missing his friends? What if there are more traps out there that we didn't see?"

Emily flopped down onto the sofa. "I know," she said. "I've been wondering the same thing. But Ally will help us find out."

There was a knock on the door, and Ally came in with four steaming mugs of hot chocolate and a plate of golden pancakes.

"This is Ally, everyone," said Emily.

"Your Majesties!" said Ally, smiling. "I saw you walking across the garden a few minutes ago, so I sent another maid to get those slippers. Is there anything else that you need?"

"We need your help, Ally," Emily told her, taking a big slurp of hot chocolate. "We need to learn how to be ninjas."

"Emily!" warned Ally. "That part of my life was a long time ago, and I don't talk about it these days."

"You can trust these princesses. Honestly, you can!" promised Emily, and the other princesses nodded.

"Do you know lots of ninja moves?" Lulu asked eagerly.

"Did it take you long to learn them?" added Jaminta.

Ally pulled up a chair, her face serious. "Learning ninja skills takes lots of patience and hours of practice. But why do you want to know? What do you want to be ninjas for?"

"We think that someone's trying to trap

the deer in Mistberg Forest without King Gudland finding out about it," said Emily.

"But why?" Clarabel burst out. "Why are they doing it?"

"Maybe they want to catch a stag to take his antlers?" said Lulu. "That kind of thing used to happen where I live. Poachers came to trap animals for horns or antlers. We've driven those people out of our kingdom now."

"So you want to find out if there are more traps?" asked Ally.

"Yes," said Emily. "We also want to find out who's leaving them."

Ally tightened her lips. "They're probably doing it at night so that no one sees them. It'll be dangerous out there."

"But if we can move around the forest without anyone seeing us, we'll be fine," said Emily. "We need to be ready to go out there tonight. Tomorrow's our last day here, the day of the Grand Ball. After that it will be too late. You will help us, won't you, Ally?"

Ally smiled. "Well, Your Majesties!" she said with a bow. "It just so happens that you've asked exactly the right person."

Ten minutes later, Ally and the princesses stood on the castle lawn. The girls had swapped their long dresses for tank tops and skirts in light colors.

Emily's pink top sparkled with silver thread and she'd pulled her red curls back into a ponytail.

"Don't we need to be camouflaged?" asked Jaminta.

"Not always," Ally told her. "I learned ninja skills from an old master when I trained as an undercover agent many years ago. You have to blend in, wherever you are and whatever you're wearing. You have to be swift and cunning."

"So, how do we practice?" asked Lulu, eager to get started.

"Well, there's your target." Ally jerked her head toward the other side of the garden, where the four princes were playing soccer. Prince Samuel's orange vest lay on the grass near the goal. "Get that vest and bring it back here without being seen."

"That's impossible!" declared Jaminta. "They're going to see us."

"I'll go first! Let me try!" said Lulu, her eyes gleaming.

The other princesses sat down on the grass to watch. Lulu put on her dark sunglasses and sneaked toward the princes using the cover of nearby bushes.

She used her acrobatic skills, running and diving into a forward roll to keep herself hidden. But when she got closer, the tallest prince saw her and waved.

Lulu came back, grinning. "I was so close! Who else wants to try?"

First Jaminta, then Clarabel, tried to reach the vest. But they, too, were spotted at the very last moment.

Emily's heart thumped faster. Silently, she tiptoed across the grass and crouched behind a stone statue of a horse and rider. She peeked around the corner of the statue. The boys were only a short distance away across the grass, but there was nothing else to hide behind.

How could she reach the vest without being seen? Then she heard sniffing behind her. Denny the dog was exploring the garden.

"Here, boy!" whispered Emily.

Denny came bounding over. Emily quickly searched for something to throw.

There was a stick on the ground nearby. It was small, but it would have to do.

"Denny," she hissed, lobbing the stick high over the grass. "Fetch!"

Denny galloped after the stick, right through the princes' game of soccer.

Emily seized her moment. She sneaked across the grass, snatched the vest, and returned to the safety of the statue. The boys were too busy looking at Denny to notice.

"Good job!" said Ally approvingly as Emily returned with the vest.

"I was lucky." Emily laughed. "I had some help from Denny!"

"A good ninja uses whatever they can find," said Ally.

Just then, the smell of sausages floated toward them.

"They started the barbecue," said Ally.

"Why don't I give you some more ninja training after lunch?"

"Great idea!" agreed Lulu.

But as the princesses walked over to the courtyard where the barbecue was cooking, a wail sliced through the air.

"My vest! It's gone!" cried Prince Samuel.

Emily made a face. "Oh, I forgot! I should take it back." She ran across the lawn and handed the orange vest over.

"What were you doing with my vest?" moaned Samuel.

"Nothing. It's completely clean," said Emily. "Sorry, I didn't mean to upset you. I won't borrow it again."

Prince Samuel's face puckered like a squeezed plum. "Mother was right," he said. "You princesses are nothing but trouble!"

CHAPTER EIGHT

Moonlight in the Forest

By the end of the day, the princesses had learned how to spot good hiding places, how to blend in with their surroundings, and how to slip in and out of rooms unseen.

The only mishap had been when Lulu crept into the kitchens and surprised the cook so much that he had dropped the gigantic raspberry cake he was holding. It had splattered across the floor in a large, sticky mess. However, once the princesses had helped him clean up, he had willingly forgiven them.

Emily smiled as she got ready for the evening banquet. The plan was a good one. They would sneak into the forest and hide there until they discovered who was laying the traps. Then they would tell King Gudland. Once he found out what was really happening, the deer would be safe again.

After a splendid dinner that the princesses were too excited to eat, they slipped out of the Banquet Hall one by one. Then they all gathered in Emily's room, having exchanged their ball gowns for dark tops and black velvet pants.

"These pants will be much easier to climb trees in," said Emily. "Is everyone ready?"

"Yes!" said Lulu and Jaminta.

Even Clarabel nodded, although she looked a little pale.

Four princess shadows flitted down the stairs and out the back door by the kitchens. They reached the golden gates for the second time that day and paused. The moon shone down, turning the forest a beautiful silver.

"We have to stay together all the time," whispered Emily.

The others nodded.

They walked stealthily toward a huge oak tree, avoiding twigs that would crack and snap, the way Ally had shown them.

Emily had noticed the oak tree earlier that day. It had branches low enough to climb up on and plenty of room to hide four princesses.

Pulling themselves up, they climbed from branch to branch. Then they tucked their legs in carefully and prepared to watch and listen, unseen.

Jaminta's bright emerald bracelet was tucked deep inside her pocket. Everything had to stay completely dark.

For a long time, there was nothing. Just the hooting of an owl and the scuffling of a little creature on the ground. Lulu shifted impatiently.

"Stay still," hissed Jaminta. "You're wobbling the whole branch!"

Then, far in the distance, a tiny light bobbed up and down. It disappeared for a moment and then returned again. As it grew bigger, they heard the rhythm of footsteps and the murmur of a voice.

The princesses froze like little mice when a cat passes by. At last the light came close enough for them to see its owner. Two dark figures walked along together, stopping here and there to put something down on the ground.

"They're setting more traps," whispered Emily.

The two figures crunched closer, grumbling as low branches caught their heads. They stopped right underneath the princesses' oak tree.

The girls held their breaths.

"How many more do we have to do?" said a man's voice.

"Two more," replied another man. "Then we've put down all ten of them."

Emily let out a gasp, then covered her mouth with her hand. She remembered seeing the men before.

"Did you hear that?" asked one man.

"Hear what? Nothing's coming near us while you're stomping along like a giant elephant," said the other. "Come on."

It seemed like forever until the men moved away. When their light had disappeared completely, the princesses

clambered down and dropped one by one onto the soft earth.

"We have to find King Gudland right now!" said Clarabel, her face pale. "Lots more deer could get trapped."

"I've seen those men before," said Emily. "They were the ones inside Duke Raven's room when I went in there by accident."

"Ready, everyone?" Jaminta got her emerald bracelet out of her pocket to light the way. "Watch your feet! Those traps could snap shut on us just as easily as on a deer."

They ran as fast as they dared back past the golden gates and into the castle garden. Long shadows streamed behind them in the moonlight.

Quickening their pace, they sped over the lawn, across the courtyard, and through the back door, reaching the entrance to the Banquet Hall, hearts drumming.

The Banquet Hall was empty, the plates and dishes from dinner already cleared.

"They must be in the drawing room," said Lulu.

They raced across the Banquet Hall and down another corridor toward a closed door.

"Who goes there?" Two guards in red uniforms stepped forward, blocking their way.

"We're the visiting princesses," said Emily. "We need to speak to King Gudland." In her black velvet pants and with no tiara, she suddenly realized she didn't look very much like a princess.

"All the kings and queens are taking part in the royal council meeting," said the second guard. "No one is allowed in."

"But we have to go in!" insisted Lulu. "The Mistberg deer are in danger. There are traps in the forest."

"Please let us in," begged Clarabel.

But the guards shook their heads. "Sorry, our orders are to let no one in until the meeting is over."

"When will they be finished?" asked Emily.

Jaminta answered her. "Not for a long time, I bet. My dad says those meetings go on until late into the night."

The princesses trailed back down the corridor to the Banquet Hall.

"We can't give up now. We're princesses," said Emily simply.

"We'll just have to figure it out ourselves," said Lulu, putting her hands on her hips.

They paused, thinking hard.

"I know how to make some deer noises," said Clarabel. "I can mimic their danger call to warn the deer away from where the traps are."

"And I worked on some new jewels this morning," said Jaminta. "They're diamonds that light up like magic when they're close to metal. We can use them to find the traps quickly."

Emily's eyes sparkled. "And we've got our ninja moves."

"And our acrobatics," added Lulu.

"We can do this! Let's go!" said Emily.

The princesses raced to Jaminta's room to collect the new jewels: a handful of diamonds that sparkled like stars.

Then they sprinted faster than ever toward the forest, their only thoughts for the safety of the deer. No one wanted to say it, but they all knew that the next trapped deer could be seriously hurt, or even worse.

They skidded to a stop in front of the golden gates.

The gates were closed. A huge gold padlock held them tightly together.

"What happened?" Emily gasped. "They were open a minute ago."

A shadow stepped out from behind a nearby statue. "I don't think princesses should be wandering around in the forest," said a deep voice. "They might get in my way."

The moon came out from behind a cloud and shone down on the man's face and his purple hat.

Emily's stomach lurched as she recognized who he was. "Duke Raven!" She groaned.

"Yes," said the man, with a nasty smile. "I made the servants lock these gates to keep you nosy girls out of the forest. There's no way you will get in there now."

CHAPTER NINE

Trapped

"I watched your little game on the lawn this afternoon," Duke Raven continued. "And I knew you were going to interfere with my plans."

"But we're only trying to help the deer," said Clarabel.

Emily stared at the duke. "Your plans! So that's why we saw those men in the forest. You sent them in there. You're the one trying to trap the deer. Why would you want to do such a terrible thing?"

"Deer antlers will look delightful on my palace wall," the duke sneered. "After I've chosen the best pair for myself, I'll sell the rest. Mistberg Forest deer have the most beautiful antlers in the world. They'll make me an awful lot of money." His narrow eyes glittered.

"We'll go and tell King Gudland what you're doing," said Lulu.

"He'll never believe you. I'm his cousin, and you don't have any proof. Without that, he'd never believe anything bad about me."

With an air of complete satisfaction, Duke Raven strolled back across the lawn toward the castle.

"Now what?" cried Lulu, shaking the gates angrily. They clanged loudly, but the padlock held them shut.

"Is there another way to get into the forest?" asked Emily.

Jaminta shook her head. "I don't think so. This is the only way out of the castle grounds. Unless we can climb the fence."

Lulu tried to haul herself up the wooden fence, but slipped down again right away.

"It's too high and too slippery," said Clarabel.

"We need something to climb up on," said Jaminta.

Lulu's eyes gleamed. "How about each other's shoulders?"

"Do you really think that would work?" asked Emily doubtfully. "We've never tried it before."

"I don't like being high up, but I'll try anything to help the deer." Clarabel's face was pale but determined.

They arranged themselves next to the fence and climbed unsteadily up onto one another's shoulders. Lulu, as the tallest, was at the bottom, followed by Emily, then Jaminta. Clarabel, as the shortest, was left to climb past them all to reach the very top.

"This is terrible!" she cried, after falling off for the seventh time. "I just can't balance."

Luckily, the grass underneath gave her a soft landing.

"Why don't I try?" suggested Emily, and, after a lot of wobbling, she managed to scramble past Clarabel to the top of the fence. Pushing her hair out of her eyes, she leaned down and pulled Clarabel up. Between them, they hauled up Jaminta, and finally Lulu.

They had chosen a place where a sturdy tree branch stretched across to the fence on the forest side. One by one, they scooted along the branch and down the tree trunk to the ground.

"Phew!" said Emily, as she landed on the forest floor. "I guess Duke Raven wasn't expecting us to do that."

"Duke Raven is a bad man," said Lulu stormily, and the others agreed.

They picked their way through the forest, directed by Jaminta's compass and the light from her bracelet. Then a rustling up ahead made them stop.

Something moved. It stepped into a shimmering shaft of moonlight and stood there, its antlers transformed into silver.

"Look," breathed Emily. "It's a stag."

The beautiful animal turned its head toward her, listening.

"Are we ready?" asked Clarabel. "I'll make the danger call to scare it far away."

They all nodded.

Clarabel lifted her hands to her lips and made a series of high-pitched noises.

The stag heard the sound and galloped away, his hooves echoing through the trees.

"It's working! Keep going, Clarabel," said Emily. "We'll find the traps."

Jaminta quickly handed out diamonds to Emily and Lulu, and the three of them scoured the forest floor, waiting for their diamonds to light up when they found any metal.

"Here's one!" cried Emily. Her diamond glowed, shedding its light like a forest star.

Jaminta rushed over and showed her how to spring the trap, making its deadly jaws close around a stick.

"Once the trap's sprung, it's useless," she explained. "It can't hurt an animal after that."

They rushed from place to place, hunting down the traps in the darkness.

Each princess worked fast. The silence was broken only by the snap of closing traps and Clarabel's deer calls ringing eerily though the forest.

Emily felt as if her diamond was leading her through the trees, as if it knew where she needed to go.

Each time it lit up a little brighter, and Emily sprang the trap and hurried on, trailing diamond-light behind her like stardust.

As the hint of a pink sunrise peeked through the trees, the princesses gathered around their oak tree again.

Sleepiness was starting to cloud over Emily's eyes, but she gave herself a shake. This was no time to lose concentration.

"How many traps have you found?" she asked.

"Two," replied Lulu.

"Three," said Jaminta.

"I've found four. That makes nine altogether," said Emily. "That means there's only one left to find."

"That's great!" Lulu yawned. "It can't be far away. Let's keep going."

They spread out again. Emily walked along, staring so hard at her diamond that she didn't even notice where she was going.

At last, the sparkling stone glowed white. Emily grinned. She'd found the very last trap!

A rustling made her look up. She was standing in a forest glade full of flowers and thick grass. Deer grazed quietly all around her, and there, right in the middle, was the trap.

Emily froze. The deer were everywhere, full-grown ones and babies. Any sudden movement or noise could make them run, and one might run straight into the trap.

The thought of hearing it snap shut on a deer made Emily shiver inside. She turned as slowly as she could.

"Clarabel?" she croaked. "Where are you?"

The deer raised their heads, poised to run.

"I'm right here, Emily," answered Clarabel. "I'll wait for your signal."

Step by tiny step, Emily edged toward the trap. If she could get to it, then maybe she could stop the deer from coming near it. She could keep them safe.

As she got closer, she could see how well the trap was hidden in the long grass. "Clarabel? Now!" she called softly.

Clarabel let out the deer's danger call and the animals took flight, galloping away through the trees.

Emily felt relief flood through her. She grabbed a stick and sprang the trap. Its teeth snapped shut tight, like a metal crocodile.

"We did it!" said Clarabel.

Emily picked up the closed trap and glared at it. "This is the one we're taking to show King Gudland. It's time that he knew what's been going on."

CHAPTER TEN

The Grand Ball

Ally brought a feast of pancakes and maple syrup up to Emily's room that morning. The girls were absolutely exhausted. Spending the whole night saving deer was hard work, even for princesses.

They sat around a little table, wearing gold-trimmed dressing gowns and tiaras, munching on pancakes and drinking tall glasses of peach juice.

King Gudland had been astounded

when they gave him the trap, and was shocked to hear that Duke Raven had shut the castle gates to try to stop them from rescuing the deer. Emily hadn't realized that his twinkly eyes could look so angry.

"Thank goodness for you four brave princesses. I would never have believed Duke Raven could do this if you hadn't shown me this horrible thing," he'd said, turning the trap over. "There will be no more traps in Mistberg Forest. I will figure this out once and for all." Then he had marched angrily away.

Shortly afterward, Duke Raven's carriage sped down the driveway and off of the castle grounds. The duke's face frowned from the carriage window.

"Look! Duke Raven's leaving," cried Emily, leaning over to look out of her turret.

"I bet King Gudland threw him out of the castle," said Jaminta.

"Good! That saves me from having to do it!" said Lulu, taking another pancake and a large helping of syrup.

The others giggled.

The rest of the morning was spent down at the shed, looking after the deer with the injured leg and finding vegetables for him from the kitchens.

In the afternoon, a feeling of excitement swept through the castle as the decorations went up for the Grand Ball. People rushed up and down the stairs with banners, golden tablecloths, and enormous bunches of roses.

Every dress was smoothed, every shoe was polished, and every ring, bracelet, and necklace rubbed until they sparkled.

The princesses met up in Emily's room in their ball gowns. The orchestra downstairs had already started to play, and the melody drifted right up into the West Tower.

Emily checked her pink satin dress in the mirror. Then she put on her ruby necklace, a ruby ring, and her best tiara, which was shaped like golden leaves woven together.

She turned to the others. "You know, we make a really great team."

"That's because we're really good at animal rescues!" said Lulu. "We're Rescue Princesses!"

The other princesses smiled.

"There must be lots of animals around the world that need our help," said Clarabel.

"You're right," Emily agreed, her hazel eyes shining. "If only we could get together to save them. But how can we call on each other? We won't be together all the time."

Jaminta looked thoughtful. "Maybe there is a way. I haven't tried it out yet, but I have an idea that could help us."

Just then, a trumpet fanfare sounded. The ball was about to begin. They climbed down the spiral stairs to the Banquet Hall together. Emily's long red curls bounced as she stepped down. Her pink dress with its red flowers shimmered in the light.

She glanced at her friends, looking perfect in their ball dresses and tiaras. No one would ever have thought they'd used ninja skills or scrambled over the castle fence the day before.

Jaminta wore a straight dress of dark-green silk decorated with beautiful golden thread. An emerald necklace hung around her neck, and she had brushed her dark hair till it shone. Perched on her head was a tiara bejeweled with beautiful Onica crystals.

Clarabel had to be careful not to tread on her pale-blue dress, which had a wide skirt that hung right down to her toes. Her golden hair was loose, and a sapphire gleamed around her neck, matching the sapphires in her tiara.

Lulu wore a shorter dress of bright yellow dotted with sequins, and a necklace with a beautiful yellow topaz. She stepped down the staircase swiftly, her black hair braided into tiny plaits and pinned up beautifully under a bright golden crown.

Emily's stomach began to gurgle as she continued down the stairs. There were so many people that she would have to greet and curtsy to.

The room below was crowded with kings and queens from all twenty royal

families. They wore ceremonial robes and cloaks in every shade, from the brightest red to the deepest blue.

Suddenly, the orchestra seemed deafening, and dozens of crowns glinted in the dazzling light of the chandeliers. Emily took a deep breath.

As the princesses reached the bottom, the four princes — Olaf, George, Dinesh, and Samuel — came over to stand next to them. They were also old enough to be presented at this year's Mistberg Ball.

The kings and queens began to form two long lines, taking the younger princes and princesses to stand with them. Emily watched a little princess, maybe only four years old, clinging to her mother's hand as she moved to her place in line.

When the kings and queens were ready, two long lines of royalty stretched out from the staircase. The princesses exchanged a look. This was the moment they had all practiced for.

They would have to walk between those lines and curtsy and speak to every single grown-up. They had to show that they could act exactly the way a princess should.

Emily took a deep breath and stepped forward. The first person in the line was a tall king with a beard. Emily curtsied. The king bowed.

Emily's heart rose as she went down the line. Everyone was smiling, she realized. The very last person in the line was King Gudland. When Emily curtsied, he took her hand.

"Princes and princesses, kings and queens," he said loudly. "May I have your attention?"

Everyone quieted. The other princesses came to stand next to Emily.

"We are very proud of all our young people. But I have something special to say about these four princesses."

He smiled at Emily. "We can see that these young ladies walk and curtsy beautifully. But today they proved that they have much greater talents than this. They showed us how to be brave, inventive, and kind to other creatures. They have saved many deer from terrible harm. I can only say how grateful I am to them, and how delighted I am to have them here. They will always find a warm welcome at Mistberg Castle!"

The kings and queens burst into applause.

"Now," continued King Gudland when the clapping finished, "let the Grand Ball begin!"

The orchestra struck up a fast tune, which sent Emily's feet tapping. She and the other princesses danced and laughed under the sparkling light of the chandeliers.

Trays of strawberry juice and fizzy cherry-ade were brought around, together with plates of iced cupcakes decorated with sugar crowns.

Emily noticed Prince Samuel trying to take five cupcakes before Queen Trudy pulled him away. Emily twirled and swirled until her head felt light and her feet tingled.

She smiled to see King Gudland joining in. He even tried to teach them his favorite dance move, called "The Mistberg Funky Chicken."

Prince Olaf came past, moving to the music. "Hey! Did you really rescue all those deer?"

"Yes, we did!" replied Emily.

"That was really brave," said Olaf. "Want to dance?"

"Maybe later." Emily smiled, twirling away toward her friends.

"Emily!" said her mom, taking her to one side. "Your dad and I wanted to say how proud we are of you. You did the right thing telling King Gudland about those traps, and you've made some lovely friends. We should ask the other princesses to come and visit Middingland soon."

Emily beamed. "Thanks, Mom! I'm sure they'd love to!"

At last all the cherry-ade had been drunk, and Emily's feet grew tired. As she went to say good night she saw Jaminta whispering to Lulu and Clarabel.

"What is it?" she asked.

"Can I borrow your ring? Just for one night?" murmured Jaminta.

"Of course," said Emily.

Jaminta winked. "I'll show you why tomorrow. I want it to be a surprise."

Emily took off the ruby ring, with its jewel that shone like fire, and gave it to her friend. She yawned. With a successful animal rescue and an exciting Grand Ball, this really had been the best day ever!

CHAPTER ELEVEN

The Rings and the Promise

Emily wanted to check on the little deer before she left the next day. When she reached the garden shed she found Lulu, Jaminta, and Clarabel already inside.

"Look!" said Clarabel. "Isn't it amazing?"

The deer tottered toward Emily, holding steady on his injured leg. His soft brown ears perked up as he listened to the girls, and his tail twitched.

"That's great! He's so much better," said Emily, delighted.

"I asked the gardeners to look after him when we go home," said Lulu. "And they'll take him back to the forest next week, when he's completely better."

"There's one more thing," Jaminta said, taking a velvet bag from her pocket. "Last night you all gave me your rings, and I worked really hard on them."

She handed the sapphire ring back to Clarabel, the topaz to Lulu, and the ruby to Emily. Then she put on her own emerald ring.

Emily slid her ring back onto her finger. The jewel in the middle had changed just a little. It was now heart-shaped, and it shone with a deeper fire. "Can they do something special now?" she asked.

Jaminta looked pleased. "It took me a long time, but I managed to make it work. Now they are communication rings. So if you speak into yours, we'll all hear you, no matter where we are and no matter how far away."

"Wow!" said Emily, her eyes wide.

"Thanks, Jaminta," said Clarabel.

Emily twisted the ring on her finger. "You know, there'll be a lot more animals out there that need our help. We should make a secret promise to always help an animal in trouble."

"No matter how dangerous the situation is!" added Clarabel.

Lulu grinned. "The more danger there is, the better!"

"Now that we have the rings, we can get help easily," said Jaminta. "We can call each other right away."

"No one else will know that we're really Rescue Princesses!" said Emily.

The girls stood in a circle with their

hands joined in the middle, one on top of the other.

"We promise to help all animals in trouble," said Emily.

"We promise," said the others.

The four rings glowed for a moment and Emily's heart missed a beat. Their adventures had only just begun.

Can't wait for
the Rescue Princesses' next
daring animal adventure?

The Wishing Pearl

Turn the page for
a sneak peek!

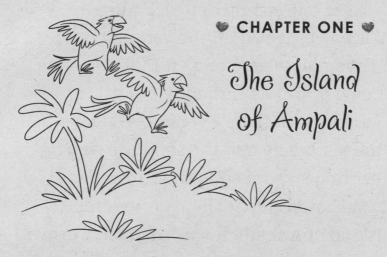

CHAPTER ONE

The Island of Ampali

Princess Clarabel scattered the last of her breakfast crumbs for the brightly colored birds that fluttered down to the veranda.

One small blue parrot sat on the wooden railing, eyeing her beadily.

"Go ahead, or there'll be none left." Clarabel laughed, and the little parrot hopped down to peck at the pieces of apricot bread as if he knew exactly what she was saying.

After one last sip of peach juice, Clarabel stepped off the veranda of the white palace onto a lawn that swept down to a clear turquoise ocean.

Her golden hair flew out behind her in the sea breeze and the sapphire ring on her finger sparkled in the sunshine.

She loved staying here on the tropical island of Ampali. It was so much warmer than her home in the kingdom of Winteria, where snow lay on the ground for most of the year.

The little blue parrot flew up to perch on her shoulder.

"Finished breakfast already?" asked Clarabel.

"Squawk!" went the parrot.

Clarabel laughed and turned her eyes back to the ocean. In the distance, a row of small ships with snowy sails was practicing for the Royal Regatta, which was happening in two days' time.

The regatta was a sailboat race and all twenty royal families from around the world had been invited to take part. Clarabel knew her father, the king of Winteria, was down at the harbor right now, watching his crew sail.

Quick footsteps sounded behind her. Three princesses came racing out of the white-walled palace, laughing as they ran. Their light summer dresses seemed to float around them.

Princess Emily had red hair and a ruby ring, Jaminta had smooth dark hair and an emerald ring, and Lulu's hair was wavy and black and she wore a ring of yellow topaz.

Clarabel's heart lifted as they came closer. She'd met them all at a Grand

Ball in the springtime. They had worked as a team to save the deer of Mistberg Forest and had become close friends at the same time. The best thing about coming to Ampali Island was seeing one another again.

"Run, Clarabel, run!" cried Lulu, her eyes sparkling.

The little blue parrot squawked and flew off Clarabel's shoulder in alarm.

Emily grabbed Clarabel's hand and whirled her away to hide behind a row of palm trees that lined the edge of the garden.

"What's going on?" asked Clarabel, trying to catch her breath.

Emily covered her mouth to stop her giggles, her red curls falling around her face.

"We're making sure Prince Samuel doesn't see us," said Jaminta. "Queen

Trudy decided that we should knit some kind of teapot covers for the Royal Regatta, so she sent him to find us and tell us to come inside."

"Teapot covers?" said Clarabel, astonished. "You must mean tea cozies. We're supposed to be making the flower garlands, aren't we?"

"I think Queen Trudy just wants to stop us from having any fun," whispered Emily. "I don't mind making the flower garlands because those will look great on the marquee, but there's no way I'm knitting those teapot things."

"I bet she wants to make us sit still all day. That's what she thinks princesses should do," said Lulu.

"Shh! Here comes Samuel," hissed Jaminta. "Remember your ninja moves, everyone."

The four princesses ducked down.

Clarabel silently went through her ninja training in her mind. Blend in with your surroundings. Wait for the right time to move. The princesses had practiced a few ninja moves in the springtime, but there was so much more to learn.

A scrawny boy with a sulky expression stepped down off the veranda. "I can't see them, Mother," he called back. "They're gone."

Slyly, he looked around him before taking a piece of paper out of his pocket. He unfolded it and held it up to the sunlight. Even from a distance, the paper looked old and frayed at the edges.